Ysgol Derwen
Higher Kinnerton

CHERRYTREE BOOKS

A Cherrytree Book

Designed by Les Dominey
Produced by
Autumn Publishing Ltd
Appledram Barns
Chichester, West Sussex

First published 1991
by Cherrytree Press Ltd
a subsidiary of
The Chivers Company Ltd
Windsor Bridge Road
Bath, Avon BA2 3AX

Copyright © Cherrytree Press Ltd 1991

British Library Cataloguing in Publication Data
Halling, Nick
  American football.
  1. Football. American
  I. Title II. Series
  796.332

ISBN 0-7451-5109-4

Printed in Singapore by Imago Publishing Ltd

All rights reserved. No part of this publication may be reproduced, stored in a retrieval system, or transmitted, in any form or by any means without the prior permission in writing of the publisher, nor be otherwise circulated in any form of binding or cover other than that in which it is published and without a similar condition including this condition being imposed on the subsequent purchaser.

Photography Allsport UK Ltd

Line drawings by Carter Beatty, West Sussex

CONTENTS

Introduction	4
Pro football in America	8
Training camp	14
Clothing and protective padding	18
Who's who in an American football club?	22
The day of the game	26
Index	32

Introduction

The object of the game

American football is a tough game of strength and stamina. It is also a game of intelligent tactics requiring quick thinking and decisive moves. So a player has to be extremely fit and strong, intelligent and agile. A lot to expect from one person! However, each player has a very supportive team of coaches and trainers behind him. Almost every move a player makes has been carefully planned, so that when he goes out on the pitch he is well-prepared for the game.

The game of American football is divided into four 15-minute quarters. However, the clock is stopped for player changeovers and half-time, which means that a match will actually last for three hours. Each side has a team of 11 players and the team that has possession of the ball is known as the offence. The teams change throughout the game according to the tactics that the head coach has planned. The offence runs with the ball or passes it down the field. The idea is to score points by getting the ball into the opposition's end zone for a touchdown (six points). An extra one point (known as a conversion) may be gained after this if the ball is kicked through the goalposts. The offence may also try to score a field goal (three points) by kicking the ball between the goalposts usually on a fourth down.

The quarterback is the field general, the man who starts the play that has been planned by the coaching staff. Good ones, like the former Dallas great, Danny White, inspire their team-mates with their qualities of leadership.

The National Football League

The National Football League (known as the NFL) is made up of 28 teams. These teams are divided into two conferences called the National Football Conference and the American Football Conference. Each conference has 14 teams and they are sub-divided into three divisions: East, West and Central.

Starting in September, the 28 teams play 16 games and from these the best teams, one from each of the six divisions, are decided.

These teams, plus six other teams with the next best records, play elimination games called playoffs. Only teams from the same conference play each other.

There is one team left from each conference after the playoffs. They meet in the last game of the season, the Super Bowl, which is held on the last Sunday in January.

Playing positions

Each player in a game of American football has a specific role and is specially trained to play in a particular position. There are various playing positions on both offence and defence but these are the most important positions in a team:

Quarterback: the field general. When play starts he shouts out coded signals that tell his team which plan of attack they are to take. On the pre-arranged code word, he takes the ball from the centre, who is one of his offensive linemen, and then carries out the planned play. He may either give the ball to a running back or throw it to a receiver.

Running back: when he has received the ball from the quarterback the running back runs with the ball as far downfield as he can without being tackled. However, when he knows the quarterback is going to pass the ball, the running back must also be ready to block players on the defence.

Wide receiver: usually the fastest man on the offence. His main role is to catch passes thrown to him and race down the field with the ball.

Offensive linemen: they protect the quarterback from the defence in passing situations. They also help to block for the running back so that he can run as far as possible downfield with the ball.

Tight end: in passing plays, when the ball is being passed downfield, he tries to get free in order to take a catch. On running plays, however, when the running back attempts to run downfield with the ball, he is expected to block defenders to help the running back.

Defensive linemen: their job is to stop the opposition's running back. In passing downs, however, they will try to tackle the opposition's quarterback before he has had a chance to throw the ball.

Linebackers: they must be alert at all times as they have to mark their opponents or support the defensive linemen on running plays. Sometimes they attack the quarterback in a surprise move called a 'blitz'.

Defensive backs: they fall into two categories, cornerbacks and safeties. The cornerbacks' main function is to cover the receivers and try to intercept the quarterback's pass. The safeties must either support the cornerbacks or move up to support the linebackers on running plays.

Defence and special teams

A professional American football squad has 45 players who play either as the offence, the defence or on special teams.

The defensive team replaces the offensive team when it loses possession of the ball. The defence's job is to try to get the ball from the opposition and prevent them from scoring. They can score two points if they manage to bring down the ball carrier of the rival team in his own end zone. This is called a safety. Other players – who appear in kicking situations, such as field goals or extra point conversions, punts or kickoffs – are called special teams.

The New Orleans Superdome in Louisiana. The field is 360 feet (110 metres) long and 160 feet (49 m) wide. White lines run across the field (gridiron) at 5 yard (4.6m) intervals. The two lines that run the length of the gridiron are called hash marks. At each end is an area 30 feet (9.1m) by 160 feet (49m), called the end zone, where touchdowns are scored.

Pro football in America

It may take as many as 10 years of hard training, gruelling effort and a lot of uncertainty before an American football player finally steps out onto the field to play in his first professional game. In the sheer excitement of this moment, however, he forgets all the pain and anxiety of the past, as he achieves his ambition to be a professional player in an American football team. This, of course, is the dream of millions of young boys, American boys particularly, but with an ever-growing following outside America.

How do they start?
American youngsters learn the basics of the game when they are still at junior high school. They learn how to pass, catch, block, and the theory of tackling. Because of the risk of serious injury to muscles and bones that are still developing, these young players are not allowed to do any actual tackling. Instead, games of touch football or flag football are played. In touch football a player is 'tackled' if he is touched two-handed by an opponent and in flag football the 'tackle' is made when the flag is pulled from the ball carrier's waist.

By the time youngsters have reached high school they know the game well and many have chosen a position they would like to play.

High school
At high school the boys learn to tackle properly and soon find out just how tough the sport can be. Those who take the game seriously must spend a lot of time practising and working on the skill required for their position. For example, those who can throw the ball the furthest will be quarterbacks and the fastest runners are usually wide receivers or defensive backs. Boys who are all-round athletes are chosen as either running backs or linebackers.

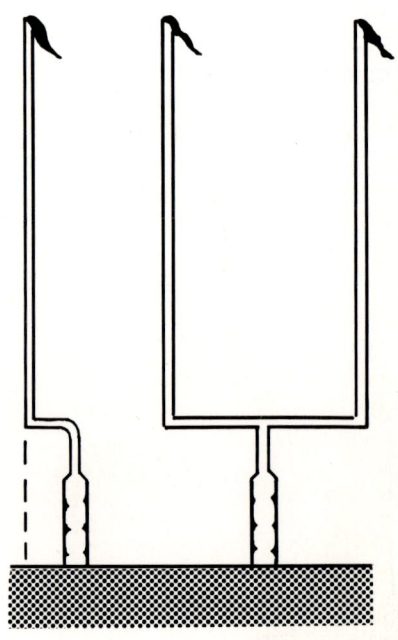

The goalposts are 20 feet (6.1 metres) high and stand over the end line. Ribbons are attached to the tops of the posts to help players determine wind strength and direction

At college

The brightest players are approached by the country's top colleges which are keen to recruit the stars of the future. In America, college sport is big business and many scholarships are granted to players who will boost the university's sporting image rather than obtain high academic grades. This does not mean it is an easy life for these gifted sportsmen. The players are expected to keep up with their studies as well as put in many hours of training.

At college level the development of a player is in the hands of his coach who decides on the position he will play. For example, a player may want to play free safety on defence, but if his coach thinks he can contribute more to the team as a wide receiver on the offence, then that is where he will play. There is no point in arguing with the coach – he has the final word!

College games

Local interest in college games is enormous and at many games there are larger crowds of spectators than at some professional games. These games are also televised and broadcast on local radio.

The college season is quite short. It runs from September to December and colleges normally play 10 or 11 games. The most successful teams are invited to play in the 15 or so end-of-season Bowl games.

The basics are drilled into would-be American football stars from a very early age. Here high school youngsters learn how to tackle correctly.

The Bowl games

Playing in a Bowl game is the highlight of a college footballer's career. These games are played between Christmas and the New Year and they attract huge local interest as well as national television coverage. To add to the atmosphere and excitement that a Bowl game creates, marching bands parade on the field and colourful and lively cheerleaders dance and chant in support of their team. More important to the players than all of the razzmatazz, however, is the presence of NFL scouts who are there to spot new talent and select their future players.

A good performance in a Bowl game has been the starting point for many great players, but for those who play badly it can put an end to all their hopes.

However, the scouts from the NFL do not make their selections solely on the results of a Bowl game. They watch the players during their college years to learn as much as possible about them, until they have a complete picture of each one. These scouts produce detailed reports on a player's on-field strengths and weaknesses, his tendency to injury, his mental toughness, as well as his behaviour away from the field. A player who lets his popularity go to his head and spends every evening celebrating with friends, for example, will be of little use to a team that wants fit, fast-thinking men in the morning.

You need more than just a pretty face to be an American football cheerleader. A head for heights can be pretty useful too!

The national college champion

With more than 160 colleges regularly playing football each year in America, it is not easy to decide who should be the national college champion, particularly as the leading contenders may not get a chance to play against each other.

The task is undertaken by selected journalists from around the country who vote for their top 20 teams. The polls are collected and the votes counted up. The college which receives the most votes is then declared to be the national champion. This system was first used in 1936, when the University of Minnesota was declared the top team in college football.

Getting drafted

Each April, the 28 teams in the NFL draft players from colleges. This means that each team picks out 12 players, and of the thousands of college players in America, only 336 of them will be given a chance to prove their skill at a team's training camp. Less than half of these will survive the sifting process at the camp, which reduces each squad to just 45 players.

Once players have been drafted to a team, they must sign a contract. When they have done this, they are regarded as professional players and earn money for playing. If a player is not drafted, he still has one more chance to get into a team. Any player can walk into a team's training camp and do his best to catch the eye of the coaching staff. Such hopefuls are called 'walk-ons' and rarely last more than a day. Some do succeed, however, and go on to become professional players.

The ball is a pointed, oval shape. It is made of a brown, grainy leather which is stretched over an inflated rubber bladder. It is 11 inches (28cm) long, 21.25 inches (54cm) around the middle, and weighs about 15 ounces (approximately 400g).

American football outside America

In the 1870s, the English game of rugby was introduced to American colleges which preferred this game to soccer. Over the years, the rules gradually changed until it became the game it is now, American football. About 100 years later American football was first played competitively in Britain.

There are more than 100 teams in Britain, divided into two leagues: the British National Gridiron League and the National League, both amateur. The season runs from April to August with 10 games in the regular season. These are followed by playoffs and end in the Bowl game in August.

The game is also played in Canada, both as an amateur status game between colleges, and professionally. The professional league is called the Canadian Football League and it is divided into two divisions, the Eastern and the Western division. Each division has four teams. The season runs from June to October with playoffs in November. The playoffs decide which teams compete for the Grey Cup, which is played for on the last Sunday in November.

Australia and New Zealand have a fast-growing following for American football, but it is played at amateur status only.

American football is played in Europe and is possibly most popular in Italy. The Italian league is split into three divisions – the first division's season ends in July with a Super Bowl, while the other two divisions play in the autumn with promotions the following spring.

Germany, France, Holland, Finland, Switzerland and Austria have had teams playing for some years and interest in the game is increasing in these countries. European club championships are held in August in a different European centre each year and teams play for the coveted Euro Bowl.

American football is popular in Europe, as well as in Japan, Australia and New Zealand. Here, the Helsinki Roosters and the Amsterdam Crusaders battle it out for the Euro Bowl, the most important club trophy in Europe.

Training camp

The players who have been drafted from college, walk-ons and veteran players (players who have had one or more year's experience in a team) all meet at a team's summer training camp, held at the end of July. This is a daunting six-week test of endurance where players are continually on trial. About 90 players arrive at the start of camp but only 45 of them will get places on the team. Competition is fierce and the future is uncertain for all but a few veteran star players.

Training and fitness

Training camps are often new sports complexes, not necessarily near the team's home base. Coaches and management tend to choose somewhere away from the distractions of any kind of night life and players are kept to a strict timetable that includes a roll call at bedtime and lights out at 10.30 pm!

Shortly after arriving at camp each player has a thorough medical examination to check that he is suitably fit, and to pinpoint any areas of weakness. Players are then given an individually structured set of exercises, involving running and weight lifting, to tone up weak muscles and bring players to peak fitness.

American football is one of the most physically demanding sports in the world. Players spend a lot of time in the fitness room where they lift weights to tone up their arm and leg muscles.

The blocking sled is an essential practice item for offensive and defensive linemen. A member of the Los Angeles Raiders learns to push his weight.

Different positions require different skills, so players are given exercises based on the demands of their position. A linebacker, for instance, spends much of his time running backwards at full speed, then suddenly changing direction. This taxing exercise is aimed at improving pass coverage skills.

The day at camp is divided into practices, meetings and meals. On the field during practice, players are shouted at by coaches, and cuts and bruises start to appear. The pressure is enormous. It is a tough time of adjustment for new players (rookies) who are no longer the stars of their college teams and have to start again at the bottom.

The playbook

Being physically gifted, however, is not enough. All NFL players have to spend at least half their time in the classroom, where they learn the team's playbook.

The club playbook is extremely important as it contains every play that the coach has planned for the coming season. Each player is expected to know, by heart, his own particular moves in any given play. Not only that, he has to know what his team-mates are doing around him. Each play is given a special name – Blue Dog 36, for instance, might be the name given to a play which indicates that a receiver has to sprint 30 yards (27.4 metres) downfield and turn sharp left. Plays are changed every week during the football season so literally hundreds of them must be learnt. All the players must be completely familiar with every play because, in game conditions when the quarterback shouts out the name during a huddle, there is no time for explanations. A player who gets it wrong or fails to understand, is of no value to his team-mates.

The cut

The moment all players dread is the cut. This is when clubs tell players who are not good enough that they must leave. There are three cut-down dates, set by the NFL. These are feared most by the players as they know the specified dates are getting closer. On these occasions the coach will ask a player to hand in his playbook and, having thanked him for his contribution, will inform him that there is not enough room for him on the team.

The final cut is made shortly before the season starts in September. It is a time of uncertainty and tension, followed by joy for those who have made it and disappointment for those who have not. The unlucky ones may try again next year, while those selected for the team have to get down to serious business – the new season.

Camp breakfast

The players are not the only ones who are busy at training camp. The catering staff have to cook three meals a day for 90 or so players, a dozen or more coaches, and various hangers-on.

Everyone, it seems, has a healthy appetite while at camp. A typical breakfast at the Tampa Bay Buccaneer training camp, for example, consists of:
10 gallons (45 litres) of milk,
4 gallons (18 litres) of orange juice,
240 eggs,
10 lbs (4.5kg) of corned beef hash,
15 lbs (6.7kg) of bacon,
9 lbs (4kg) of sausages,
8 lbs (3.6kg) of hash-brown potatoes,
5 lbs (2.2kg) of cottage cheese,
4 lbs (1.8kg) of butter,
and what seems like the contents of an entire orchard of oranges.

Exhibition games

Towards the end of camp, the players who have survived the first set of cuts have a chance to take part in pre-season exhibition games. The results of these do not count towards the final season's standings, but they produce a lot of interest as the fans gather to see how their team will look in the coming season.

The atmosphere is tense as coaches assess, often for the first time, how players cope with game conditions. A rookie who looked outstanding on the practice field, for example, may go to pieces when he is faced with the pressure of the game. On the other hand, those who have lacked sparkle in practice may do far better when faced with real opponents. It is a 'make or break' time for many players and a dropped pass, a fumble, or failure to deliver a block can result in being cut. Others establish their reputations in exhibition games and go on to enjoy success in the sport.

In camp, quarterbacks are a protected species. They wear red shirts to distinguish them from other players, and to warn defenders not to hit them.

Clothing and protective padding

Clothing
In addition to thin, knee-length pants, a player wears a T-shirt, long socks and the team shirt. The shirt has the player's name on the back and his number on the sleeves, back and front. This number tells the position of the player.

Shoes
The type of shoes players wear depends on the surface of the pitch and the playing position. Shoes worn when playing on a grass pitch have studs or cleats on the sole. Shoes worn on pitches of artificial turf are covered in small rubber nubs to give better grip on this smoother surface.

The helmet
The most important part of the body to be protected is the brain. Players wear helmets to prevent skull fractures and reduce the risk of concussion. The helmet is heavily padded and lined with energy-absorbing foam material, or plastic air bags that are inflated with a pump to give a close fit. It is vitally important that a helmet fits snugly in order to give proper protection. The helmet also has a faceguard to protect the nose and mouth and many players fit a visor for eye protection.

Every player will spend plenty of time making sure that his ankles are firmly taped for protection against sprains and breaks. It is often impossible to tell where the boot ends and the sock begins.

The helmet is probably the single most important item of equipment a player wears. The helmet helps prevent skull fractures and reduces the risk of concussion.

Miles of tape

Equipping an American football squad is big business. The average cost of kitting out an NFL team is around $300,000 (approximately £150,000) per year. The adhesive tape used to protect ankles and fingers is probably the cheapest single item of equipment a club purchases, but it is also probably the most used.

It has been estimated that the 28 NFL teams use an amazing 3640 miles (5858 km) per season. To tape a single ankle will use up to 5 yards (4.5 metres) of adhesive tape.

Pads

As anyone who has ever watched or played the game knows, American football is one of the most physically demanding sports. Players from high-school age upwards wear a lot of padding to protect themselves from the harsh battering they will inevitably experience. When they are preparing for a match, players can take up to two hours getting dressed!

The first item of protection is a girdle shell. This contains the hip pads and the spine protector. The hip pads soften the blow of a heavy shoulder tackle coming in from the side. The spine protector supports the lower spine.

Inside the playing pants are pockets for thigh pads of heavy felt covered with leather, and knee pads which have metal ribs and joints. The thigh contains the longest muscle in the body and it is easily bruised or injured. The knee is a weak joint and needs rigid protection. Players also wear a plastic box to protect the groin.

Everyone associates shoulder pads with the game of American football. These are not worn to make the players look threatening or tough, they are needed as protection from hard tackles. Players who play in positions where the most tackling takes place, such as linemen, wear larger shoulder pads than wide receivers who need to be able to dodge and run fast.

The shoulder pads are connected to a collar and chestplate which is light, but very strong. The collar, usually padded with foam, restricts the backwards and sideways movement of the head and helps prevent neck injuries. The pads over the shoulders (called epaulettes) are reinforced with plastic and protect the collarbone and shoulder blades. The chest plates at the front and back help protect the ribs and internal organs, such as the lungs.

Offensive and defensive linemen wear pads to protect the forearms and hands from the constant wear and tear of pushing against opponents. Quarterbacks, receivers, linebackers, running backs and defensive backs do not wear these as they need unrestricted use of their hands during the game.

A player in shoulder pads, collar and chestplate. He is also wearing arm and hand pads, hip pad and a girdle shell.

Atlanta Falcons' defensive back, Deion Sanders, relies on speed, so he will be one of the most lightly padded players on the team. The towel hanging from his belt is used to keep his hands and fingers free from dirt and sweat.

Who's who in an American football club?

Each NFL team is run in the same way as a major business. Although the players work mainly with their own specialist position coaches on a day-to-day basis, they also have to be aware of who's who within the overall structure. There is a lot more to an NFL team than the 45 players out on the field each Sunday.

The head coach

The head coach makes the important decisions that determine how the team will perform on the field. He is responsible for putting the playbook together, and ensuring that all his players know and understand what is expected of them. Depending on his seniority and experience, the head coach may also be involved in contract and salary negotiations.

Despite the title he is given, the head coach does not normally become too closely involved in day-to-day coaching. He sets the basic tone and policy for the team and works closely with his offensive and defensive co-ordinators. They have the responsibility of ensuring the smooth working of these two separate units.

NFL coaches like Buddy Ryan formerly of the Philadelphia Eagles need to possess a wide variety of skills. In addition to planning how the team will play on the field, another of his functions is to act as the club's spokesman to the media.

Coaches watch video film to assess individual players from rival teams and look for their strengths and weaknesses. Players also benefit from seeing their performance on film. Here Miami quarterback, Dan Marino, analyses his game and looks for potential areas of improvement.

Assistant coaches

A team usually has assistant coaches who specialize in training players in different positions. There will be a running backs coach, receivers/quarterbacks coach, offensive line coach, defensive line coach, linebackers coach, defensive backs coach, and special teams coach. There are also strength and conditioning coaches who supervise players in the weights room and with their exercises.

The general manager

The ideal general manager is someone who understands the needs of the team and coaches, and is used to dealing with a large number of people.

The general manager relies on the head coach reporting to him. If the team is not performing well on the field, and the general manager feels the fault is with a coach, he has the authority to sack the coach and hire a replacement.

It is the general manager's job to negotiate the players' contracts. When dealing with contracts there is also the question of how long a player should sign up for. Often the general manager will offer only one year's contract, particularly if a new player has still to prove himself worthy of the team.

Big names, however, especially the top quarterback, running back and wide receiver, enjoy the benefits of long-term contracts because they are players that the club does not want to lose.

The owner

Some NFL owners get involved in the day-to-day running of the club. Others take a step back and leave that kind of business to senior employees.

In all cases, though, the owner is the man with the highest authority and everyone in the organization must understand this.

He (or she, in the case of Los Angeles Rams' owner, Georgia Frontiere) is the person who pays the bills and salaries, and is responsible for the upkeep of the stadium. The owner may be wealthy enough to finance all this on his own. However, the proceeds from games, such as supporters' ticket fees, money made from the car parks and the sale of food, help to finance a club. A great deal of money also comes from television and radio contracts.

The officials or 'zebras' at an NFL game come from a variety of backgrounds, but all are part-timers, with regular jobs during the week.

Medical staff

American football is a tough sport and for this reason all clubs employ medical staff including a doctor, physiotherapist and a dentist. No team ever goes through a season without a few injuries and it is the medical staff's job to get players back on their feet and ready to play again as soon as possible.

Each NFL team enjoys the support of a fully-qualified medical staff. The contents of this medical box are typical of the equipment used to treat minor injuries.

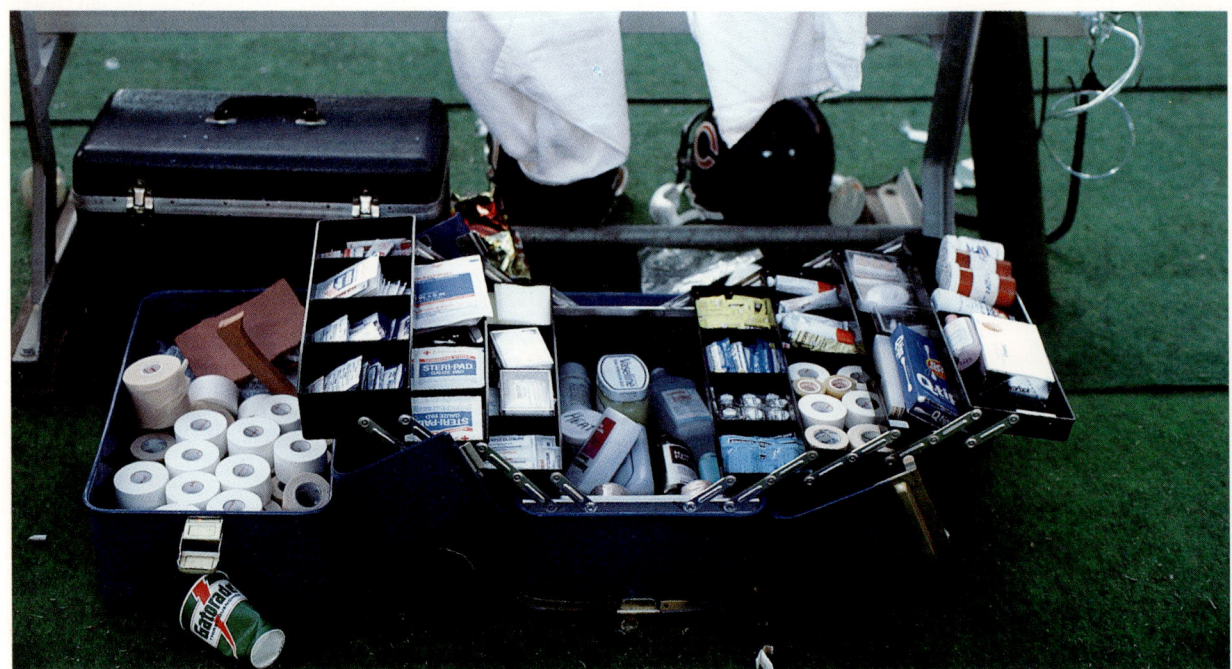

Officials

A game of American football would not work without officials to control it, and to the players, they are some of the most important people outside the club.

There are seven officials at a game: an umpire, head linesman, a line judge, a back judge, side judge, field judge and a referee, who is generally in charge. These officials each have a flag – a yellow piece of cloth with a weight in one corner. If an official sees a rule being broken, he throws this flag down onto the pitch.

The officials all wear black and white shirts which accounts for the nickname of 'zebra'.

The day of the game

At the game

Most NFL games take place on Sunday afternoons, although some are played on Sunday night, and one fixture per week takes place on Monday night for two of the 28 teams.

On the day of the game, the players and coaches meet at the team's offices in the morning to check last-minute preparations. The players have a light lunch before going to the locker rooms where their clothes and pads are laid out by the club's equipment manager.

The players

About an hour before the kickoff, the coach leads the players onto the field for warm up exercises. The players are able to loosen their muscles and, at the same time, get a feel for the playing surface and the atmosphere inside the stadium.

For the American football fan, game day is an excuse for a long party. Many fans will arrive at the ground several hours before kickoff to enjoy a tailgate party.

The spectators

Crowds of excited, good-natured supporters will already be in their seats. They arrive wearing hats, sweatshirts, T-shirts, large foam hands, all in their team's colours to show their loyalty and support. Some meet friends in the car park and have barbecues beside their cars. These are known as 'tailgate' parties. (Tailgate is the American word for the hatchback door of an estate car.) Marching bands parade on the pitch and lively cheerleaders go through their routines to unite their team supporters. The queues for popcorn, hot dogs and hamburgers constantly form and reform, and the smell of food wafts across the stadium throughout the game.

Back to the players

After the warm up exercises, the players troop off the pitch and return to the locker room where they wait anxiously for the start of the game. During these moments the coach will lead the players in a team prayer, a moment of unity and calm that is respected by Christians and non-Christians alike. The prayer is not for victory or personal gain, but that everyone plays as well as they can and that no one gets hurt.

Marching bands entertain the crowd before kickoff and also during the half-time interval.

The signal to come back onto the pitch is given and it is time for the real business of the day to begin. The players emerge from the tunnel into a seething cauldron of noise: this is what the crowds have been waiting for. The players' spirits rise as they hear the cheers. Supporters chant the name of their favourite player and if he acknowledges them with a wave, the place erupts with wild, enthusiastic cheers. The teams welcome the encouragement from the crowds and appreciate their support. The offensive or defensive players of both teams and their head coaches are introduced to the fans by name over the loudspeaker.

The team captains meet in the middle of the field for the pre-game toss. The kickoff team lines up against the kick return unit of the opposition and when the referee blows his whistle, the kicker boots the ball as far as he can into the opposition's half of the field. The game has started.

All the preparation, the rigours of training camp, the punishing routine to get to full fitness, the hours spent learning the playbook and glued to the video machine, will prove worthwhile in the next three hours.

When the game is over the winning team will be overjoyed and needless to say, the supporters will be ecstatic. A perfect end to a wonderful day for some

The Super Bowl

The Super Bowl is one of the world's great sporting occasions. In America, the players and coaches have to face much pre-game analysis in the week leading up to the game. The press, radio and television devote a lot of time and space to questioning whether or not a certain player's last performance qualifies him to be in the team; or whether another player's injuries will stop him playing; as well as discussing and arguing about a team's chances of winning.

The Super Bowl often draws the largest viewing figures of any programme on television. Interest in the game outside America has expanded too. At Super Bowl XXIV in January 1990, there were more than 200 foreign journalists present. Many countries televise the Super Bowl live, despite the fact that, because of time differences, viewers in some countries have to wait until the early hours of the morning to watch the game. In fact, this also happens with different States in America.

supporters. For the players, a win on Sunday means that the club's offices will be a happy place to be for the week. The coaches are pleased and the players will look forward to reliving their victory when a video of the game is shown in the film room.

Defeat, however, hangs over a losing club like a dark cloud. Their supporters are disappointed, the media want to know what is wrong with the team and the pressure on coaches and players to win the next match is intense. Such emotions are short-lived, however, for there is another match to prepare for and a lot of work to be done before next week's game. No matter what, their loyal supporters will be there to cheer them on to possible victory next time.

A play in action. The offence (in red) has just snapped the ball, and the quarterback is handing it to a running back. The offensive linemen are pushing the defensive players back in order to allow the running back space to run with the ball.

Glossary of terms

Down
Each move in American football starts from a fixed situation called a 'down'. The offence has four downs (attempts) to move the ball 10 yards (9.1m) down the pitch. If the team succeeds in four or less downs they get another 'first down' and four more attempts to move a further 10 yards. If they fail, they can either punt the ball away to the opposition or try to kick a field goal through the posts at the back of the end zone.

Upfield, downfield
When the team with the ball is in its own half of the pitch, its players are said to be moving upfield. When they are running towards the end zone in the other team's half, they are moving downfield.

Blocking
Offensive players try to stop the other team from getting the ball by running in front of them and blocking their way.

Kickoff
The game is started by a kickoff, when one team places the ball on a tee on their own 35 yard-line and kicks it to the opposition. After a team has scored this process is repeated.

Play
The offence's planned attack when they have the ball.

Standings
The equivalent of rankings or league tables. The teams with the best records are at the top of the standings, while those with the worst are at the bottom.

Kick return unit
The kick return unit is the group of 11 players who get the ball after the kickoff and try to run with it towards the opposition.

Playbook
The coach's manual which contains all the team's plays.

Tackling
Bringing down a ball carrier by knocking him to the ground or preventing him from moving forward. A player is considered tackled when one knee hits the ground.

Trade
The transfer of one player from one team to another.

Huddle
Before each play, the offence gather in a tight group to listen to what they are going to do next. The quarterback usually gives the instructions.

Pass coverage
The defensive team's plan to prevent passing plays by keeping their opponents closely marked.

Punt
The ball is drop-kicked away to the other team, generally when the offence has failed to move the ball 10 yards in a down.

The highlight for any team is an appearance in the Super Bowl. Beside the Super Bowl trophy are helmets from the San Francisco 49ers and the Cincinnati Bengals, who played in Super Bowl XXIII.

INDEX

American Football
    Conference 4
Amsterdam Crusaders 13
assistant coaches 23
Australia 12

backs, defence 6,8,20
ball 12
blocking 6,8,30
blocking sled 15
Britain 12
British National Gridiron
    League 12

Canada 12
cheerleaders 10,27
Cincinnati Bengals 31
clothing 18
coaches 4,9,14,15,17,22,29
college 9
    Bowl games 10
    games 9
    season 9
contracts 23
conversion 4,7
cornerback 6
cut 16,17

defence 7
dentist 24,
down 4,30,31
downfield 6,16,30
draft system 12

Eastern Football
    Conference 12
end zone 7,13
equipment manager 26
Euro Bowl 13
Europe 13
European club
    championships 13
exhibition games 17

field goal 4
film and video 28
flag football 8

general manager 23
girdle shell 20
goalposts 4,8
Grey Cup 12
gridiron 7

hash marks 7
head coach 4,22,23,28
helmet 18
Helsinki Roosters 13
high school 8
huddle 16,31

injuries 24
Italy 13

Japan 13

kickoff 7,26,28,30
kick return unit 28,30

linebackers 6,8,15
linemen, defence 6,20,29
linemen, offence 6,20
Los Angeles Raiders 15

marching bands 10,27
Marino, Dan 23
media coverage 10
medical staff 24

National College
    Champion 10
National Football
    Conference 4
National Football
    League 4,16,19
        games 4,26,28
        scouts 10
        season 4
National League 12
New Orleans Superdome 7
New Zealand 12

offence 4,31
officials 24,25
owner 24

pads 20,26
pass coverage 15,31
Philadelphia Eagles 22
physiotherapist 24
play 6,15,16,30
playbook 15,16,22,28,31
playoffs 4,12
punt 7,31

quarterback 4,6,8,16,17,20,
    23,29,31

referee 25
rookies 15,17
running back 6,8,20,23
Ryan, Buddy 22

safety 6,7,9
Sanders, Deion 20
San Francisco 49ers 31
shoes 18
shoulder pads 20
special teams 7
standings 17,30
Super Bowl, game 4,13,28
    trophy 31
supporters 27,28,29

tackling 8,9,20,31
tailgate party 26,27
Tampa Bay Buccaneers 16
tape 18,19
tight end 6
touchdown 4,7
touch football 8
training camp 12,14,28
    breakfast 16

University of Minnesota 10
upfield 30

veteran 14

walk-ons 12
Western Interprovincial
    Football Union 12
White, Danny 4
wide receiver 6,8,20,23